MW01608924

My Spin Around Dress

by Diana Holt

illustrated by Ane M. Galego

Order this book online at www.trafford.com/07-1333
or email orders@trafford.com

Most Trafford titles are also available at major online book retailers.

© Copyright 2007 Diana Holt, illustrations by Ane M. Galego.
All rights reserved. No part of this publication may be reproduced, stored in a retrieval
system, or transmitted, in any form or by any means, electronic, mechanical, photocopying,
recording, or otherwise, without the written prior permission of the author.

Note for Librarians: A cataloguing record for this book is available from Library
and Archives Canada at www.collectionscanada.ca/amicus/index-e.html

Printed in Victoria, BC, Canada.

ISBN: 978-1-4251-3458-7

*We at Trafford believe that it is the responsibility of us all, as both individuals
and corporations, to make choices that are environmentally and socially sound.
You, in turn, are supporting this responsible conduct each time you purchase a
Trafford book, or make use of our publishing services. To find out how you are
helping, please visit www.trafford.com/responsiblepublishing.html*

*Our mission is to efficiently provide the world's finest, most comprehensive
book publishing service, enabling every author to experience success.
To find out how to publish your book, your way, and have it available
worldwide, visit us online at www.trafford.com/10510*

www.trafford.com

North America & international
toll-free: 1 888 232 4444 (USA & Canada)
phone: 250 383 6864 ♦ fax: 250 383 6804
email: info@trafford.com

The United Kingdom & Europe
phone: +44 (0)1865 722 113 ♦ local rate: 0845 230 9601
facsimile: +44 (0)1865 722 868 ♦ email: info.uk@trafford.com

10 9 8 7 6 5 4 3 2 1

I would like to dedicate this book firstly to my children,

Don, Randy and Tim

They have been with me through thick and thin, and have shared all phases and challenges with me. Thank you boys, I love you!!

Secondly, to all of my

Grandchildren and Great Grandchildren

who have given me more joy, fun and memorable moments in my life than they know. They have taught me to love, laugh hard and often, and to find delight in the simplest of things.

Thank You

To My Children
for letting me enjoy the Grandchildren often.

Never would I have experienced the excitement that they enjoyed otherwise. I got to see them grow up and feel the joy of each stage of their changes, which makes it possible to share with them the pleasures of today.

Ane Galego
for doing such an excellent job of the illustrations.

A Special Thank You
to my many friends
for their endless continual encouragement.

Thank You to God
for being with me throughout my life, and never giving up on me. My work would never have been completed without God's help.

I always have the feeling of Happiness
When I am wearing my
'Spin Around Dress'.

When I am out at play
In my jeans and my vest,
        I run around and do my best,
But, I always feel 'Great'
        In my 'Spin Around Dress'!

When I am comfortable and warm,

I can weather a storm.

But I still feel my best,

In my 'Spin Around Dress'!

Now I have found that,

    When I spin round and round,

I get dizzy and I fall to the ground.

    And I feel so blessed,

To be in my 'Spin Around Dress'!!

When I put on my Spin Around Dress,

I feel like a Queen or a Princess.

I can sing, and I can dance,
I can whistle, and I can prance.

My heart feels full,
and I can do my very best,

If I am wearing 'My Spin Around Dress'!!

If I am playing with my friends,
Or just taking a rest,
I still feel my best,
In my 'Spin Around Dress'.

I always feel blessed in my

'SPIN AROUND DRESS'.